THE D.O.G.

A *Lola Jones* BOOK

JONATHAN EIG

illustrated by
ALICIA TEBA GODOY

ALBERT WHITMAN & CO.
Chicago, Illinois

For Sydney Jackson—JE

A mis padres—ATG

ecce

Library of Congress Cataloging-in-Publication data
is on file with the publisher.

Text copyright © 2021 by Jonathan Eig
Illustrations copyright © 2021 by Albert Whitman & Company
Illustrations by Alicia Teba Godoy
Hardcover edition first published in the United States of America
in 2021 by Albert Whitman & Company
Paperback edition first published in the United States of America
in 2021 by Albert Whitman & Company
ISBN 978-0-8075-6570-4 (hardcover)
ISBN 978-0-8075-6572-8 (paperback)
ISBN 978-0-8075-6573-5 (ebook)

Printed in the United States of America
10 9 8 7 6 5 4 3 2 1 LB 24 23 22 21 20

Design by Aphelandra

For more information about Albert Whitman & Company,
visit our website at www.albertwhitman.com.

TABLE OF CONTENTS

1. The Witching Hour 1

2. Ten Dollars.. 5

3. Phooey to Rules 10

4. Doodle Dreams 23

5. M Is for Mocha... 31

6. Artful Dreams... 41

7. Hatching a Plan 50

8. A Black-and-White Dog Appears...Again!...56

9. The D.O.G. 64

10. True Friends Are Like Fingers.................. 68

11. Hot Diggity Dog!.. 78

12. Going Home... 83

MEET Lola Jones AND FRIENDS

Hi! I'm Lola.
I love books and
I love adventure.
When I'm trying
to solve a problem,
I know I can count
on my family, my
friends, and characters
from my favorite books!

Lola Jones

Grampa Ed
I'm Lola's grandfather.
That kid cracks me up.
I try to pretend I'm
grumpy sometimes,
but she never
falls for it.

Lillian Jones
I'm Lola's mother.
I love playing soccer
and having crazy
dance parties with
my daughter.

Mrs. Gunderson
I'm Lola's teacher,
and I love my third
graders. My favorite
book is *Charlotte's
Web* by E.B. White.

Maya and **Fayth**
We're Lola's best friends.
Whatever wild plan she's hatching,
we're always there to help out!

1.
The Witching Hour

Lola Jones sat straight up in her bed.

She looked around for the dog that had just barked and jumped on top of the covers, waking her up. But it wasn't there. She looked under the covers. She looked under her pillow and on the floor. She even leaned over, upside down, to look under the bed.

No dog.

Lola sat still and listened carefully. No sound of paws on the wooden floor of her room. No more barking.

The dog had been a dream!

Lola snuggled back under the covers and shut her eyes. Maybe, if she went back to sleep, she'd keep dreaming about the cute little black-and-white dog jumping up and licking her face and begging her to play. But she just couldn't fall asleep again.

Lola liked noise when she went to sleep—the sound of footsteps from the apartment above, the hum of a television, which her mother watched at night, the rumble of cars and trucks on the street. She wasn't used to such quiet. Lola sat up again and saw herself in the mirror. She was eight and a half years old. Her hair was brown, her eyes were brown, and she had big dimples. She was small for her age, but fast and strong and smart.

Pale light came in through the window blinds. She looked at the clock: 5:21 a.m. Too early to get up. Is this what the character Sophie referred to as the witching hour in Lola's new favorite book, *The BFG*? In *The BFG*, the witching hour is a special time in the middle of the night when every person is in such a deep sleep that giants come out and do wild, giant things.

Lola didn't believe there was a *real* witching hour. She knew that buses and trains ran all night in Chicago, and she knew that her favorite restaurant, Stella's Diner, stayed open 24 hours.

But, still...

Lola stood up on her bed, parted the slats of the window blinds, and peeked out. There were no witches or giants, only the side of a red brick building, a patch of pale sky above, and a sliver of sidewalk below. Boring. There wasn't even a way to tell it was springtime.

But then Lola heard a sound from outside.

Footsteps?

Too soft.

Too tippy-tappy.

She raised the blinds and pressed her cheek against the cool glass of her bedroom window to get a better angle. The tippy-tappy sound grew louder. Not loud, but louder, a *tiny* bit louder.

And that's when she saw it, or thought she saw it.

It was a little dog!

No leash.

No owner.

Just a dog.

A cute little black-and-white dog!

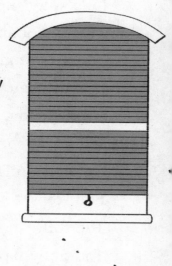

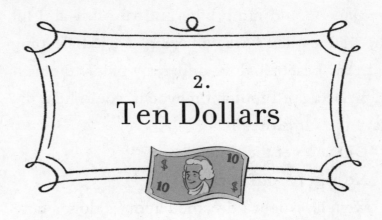

2.
Ten Dollars

"Grampa, did you ever have a dream that you wished would come true?"

Lola sat cross-legged on the floor, reading *The BFG* while Grampa Ed sat in a chair and bent over to tie her hair in pigtails. Today he was using orange hair ties and making Lola's head look like a grove of tangerine trees. He paused, slurped from his coffee cup, and went back to work on the pigtails.

"Oh, sure," he said. "When I was a kid, I dreamed that I played centerfield for the White Sox, and I caught every ball hit my way. I was *smooth*. I could jump high and run fast and hit the ball a mile. I was amazing! I tried sleeping with my baseball glove under my pillow the next night because I thought maybe it would help me have the same dream."

"Did you get the same dream?"

"No, I got a stiff neck."

"Well, last night I dreamed about a dog, a cute little black-and-white dog," Lola said, "so maybe that means I'm going to get one! I even woke up and saw a black-and-white dog out the window in the alley. That must be a sign!"

"Did I ever tell you about *my* dog?" Grampa Ed slurped more coffee. Grampa Ed had white hair, a white beard, and a big belly. On his left bicep he had a tattoo that read *Whatever Lola Wants*. He lived in an apartment on the first floor. Lola and her mother lived on the second floor.

"*Whoopsey-splunkers*, Grampa! You never told me you had a dog! I can't believe you would leave out such an important detail of your life story!"

"*Whoopsey what?*"

"*Whoopsey-splunkers!* It's from this book." Lola held up *The BFG*. "It means *wow!*"

"Oh." Grampa shrugged. "Well, I probably didn't tell you because we didn't have the dog too long. Your uncle Matt found him one day in an alley. The little pooch was small and sad. Uncle Matt and I hid him in our room and took care of him. We never told our parents because there were no dogs allowed in our apartment building."

"Oh, Grampa! I have a million and one questions! What was the dog's name? Was he cute? Was he a labradoodle?

Or a goldendoodle? Those are my two very favorite dogs! Was he smart? Did he do any tricks? Did you get to keep him? What was the dog's name? Wait…did I already ask that?"

Grampa Ed put down the hairbrush and the big bag of elastic hair bands and tapped Lola gently on the top of her head. That was his signal that he was done making pigtails.

"Let's finish getting ready for school. I'll tell you on the way."

"Just tell me the name of your dog before we go!" Lola stood up and turned to face Grampa Ed. She smiled, and her dimples appeared. "Just the name! *Please*!"

"Ten Dollars," he said.

"You want me to pay you to tell me the dog's name? Grampa, you *know* I don't have that much money!"

Grampa Ed laughed. His big chest and tummy went up and down.

"No, no. That's what Matt and I called the dog. Ten Dollars. We thought that when the owner finally came to get his dog, we'd get a big reward for finding him. Ten Dollars!"

"So, what happened to Ten Dollars? Did you get to keep him?" Lola waited.

"I'll tell you on the way to school."

"Awww!"

"Let's go to school, kid!"

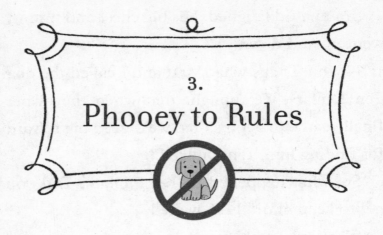

3.
Phooey to Rules

Lola and Grampa Ed stopped at Lola's friend Maya's house first, and then they went to Fayth's house. Grampa Ed walked the girls to school almost every day. Along the way, Lola told her friends about her dream. The girls got so excited that Lola forgot to ask Grampa Ed about his dog.

"It's a sign!" Maya said.

"It's an omen!" Fayth said.

"I know!" Lola said. "That's what I thought, too!"

"You're getting a dog!" Maya shouted.

"For your birthday!" Fayth shouted.

"But Lola's birthday is in August," Maya said, "and it's only April!"

Maya and Fayth had dogs, and Lola didn't think it was fair that she couldn't have one, too. But Lola's mother said their apartment was too small, no one was home all day to walk a dog, and pets were expensive. Even if they wanted one, their apartment building had a rule: No Dogs Allowed.

"Oh, I really do hope I get a dog—now or for my birthday," Lola said. "But...our building has a rule."

"Phooey to rules!" Maya said.

"Yeah, phooey to rules!" Fayth agreed.

"Rules are meant to be broken!" said Maya. "Guess who said that?"

"Who?" Lola asked.

"I don't know," said Maya, "but probably someone who got famous for breaking rules!"

ello

At a quarter past eight Lola and her friends settled into their seats in Mrs. Gunderson's classroom. A warm spring breeze blew gently through the open windows and fluttered the classroom's flag.

"Good morning, scholars," Mrs. Gunderson said, her voice cheerful as always. "Before we begin our poetry unit, I'm going to pass out these permission slips for next week's field trip. We'll be visiting the animal shelter. Please ask your parents or guardians to sign this."

Lola's eyes opened wide. She looked at Maya and then at Fayth.

Lola whispered: "The animal shelter!" She couldn't believe it.

Maya whispered back: "It's a sign!"

Fayth whispered: "Another omen!"

"Girls," Mrs. Gunderson said patiently. "Time for poetry, please."

Lola had a difficult time concentrating on poetry. She had dogs on her mind. Big dogs. Little dogs. Black dogs. White dogs. Labradoodles. Goldendoodles. Schnoodles. A dog named Ten Dollars. Maybe her dream really *had been* a sign!

Mrs. Gunderson gave everyone fifteen minutes to write a poem about spring. The poems didn't have to rhyme, she said, but they had to include *figurative language*. Figurative language, Mrs. Gunderson explained, was like fancy clothing. It was a way of dressing up your writing by saying something indirectly and creatively. Lola wasn't sure if she was getting the hang of it or not, but she looked out the window at the  window boxes filled with blooming flowers and started to write.

After fifteen minutes, Mrs. Gunderson asked a few students to read their poems. Lola was one of them.

"Um, do I have to?"

"Yes, please." Mrs. Gunderson smiled.

Lola cleared her throat.

"Um, O.K. My poem is called 'Woof Woof for Spring.'"

Spring raced like a labradoodle.

It licked my face like a jumpy schnoodle.

Spring chased a baseball in the park.

Spring woke me up with a cute little bark.

"That's very nice figurative language," Mrs. Gunderson said. "Spring can be a lot like a puppy, and you captured it well, Lola."

Normally, Lola would have been happy as a dog with a bone to earn Mrs. Gunderson's praise. But her excitement about dogs was beginning to wash away like sidewalk chalk in the rain. It was fun to dream about dogs, and fun to rhyme about them, too. But what was the point if she could never have a *real* dog?

Lola thought about Sophie in *The BFG*. Sophie got stuck in a giant's cave for a long time, and she never got discouraged. She remained patient and curious and optimistic. If Sophie could do it, Lola could do it, too!

Lola and Grampa Ed were setting the table for dinner when Lola heard the doorknob turn. She ran down the hall and wrapped her mother in a hug before Lillian Jones could even set down her keys.

"Ooooh, what a strong hug!" Lillian Jones squeezed Lola back and kissed her cheek. "Want to help me make dinner?"

"Sure! Want to hear the poem I wrote in school today?"

"Sure! Let me say hello to Grampa first."

Lillian Jones gave her father a kiss on the

cheek and washed her hands. She arranged the ingredients for dinner on the kitchen counter: eggs, cheese, avocado, red peppers, tortillas, and butter. They were having one of Lola's favorite dishes: quesadillas with cheese, avocado, and grilled pepper on the inside, with a fried egg on top.

Lola recited her poem to her mother as she chopped peppers.

"That's a fun poem, Lola," Lillian Jones said. "Could you please hand me the cayenne pepper, sweetie?"

Lola reached over to the spice rack and picked up a jar. "The BFG has jars in his kitchen, too," Lola said. "Lots! But instead of spices, they're full of dreams."

"Oh, how interesting!" Lillian Jones said.

"My spice rack would be full of *dog* dreams," Lola said. "Like my poem. It's called 'Woof Woof for Spring' because it has a lot of dog stuff in it."

"I picked up on that right away," Lillian Jones said, smiling.

"Because I had a dream about a dog last night."

"Uh-huh."

"Because I *really* want a dog."

"Uh-huh."

"Because my class is taking a field trip to the animal shelter and maybe I'll find a cute dog there and I can have one, right?"

"Uh...no."

Lola's shoulders sagged.

"Aww, Mom, why not?"

"I've told you before, Lola. I don't think it's a good fit for us. And it's against the building rules, anyway."

"But, Mom! Rules were meant to be broken! Someone famous said that!"

Lola's mother turned from the kitchen counter and stared at Lola. "Um, sweetie, you do know that I'm a police officer, right?" Lola nodded. "So," Lillian Jones said, splitting a pepper slice in half and giving one half to Lola and crunching the other half herself, "rules were meant to be *enforced*." Lillian smiled at Lola. "Your mother said that."

At dinner, Grampa Ed told the story of the dog named Ten Dollars that he and his brother Matt hid in their room. He said he and Matt took good care of Ten Dollars. They taught Ten Dollars to shake hands and catch a ball.

"When Ten Dollars started putting on weight from all the good food we sneaked him from the kitchen, he would wrestle with us for the ball. That dog was *strong*! But the stronger the dog got, the more he ate." Grampa picked up a giant wedge of quesadilla and popped it in his mouth. Right away he picked up another wedge and popped that in his mouth, too.

"That's how we got caught. Because we gave the dog a big juicy steak that was supposed to be for my mother's birthday dinner. When she asked what happened to the steak, we told her about the dog. Finally, we put up signs in the neighborhood, and a few days later, the owner came to get his dog."

"Was the owner happy to get his *kicksy* dog back?"

"His *what*?" Lillian Jones asked.

"*Kicksy*, Mom," Lola said. "It's BFG language for 'bouncy and full of energy.'"

"Oh, I see." Lillian Jones looked at Grampa Ed and smiled.

Grampa Ed smiled back and nodded. "Yes, the owner was very happy. But he didn't call the dog Ten Dollars, of course."

"What was the dog's real name?" Lola asked.

Grampa Ed picked up another quesadilla wedge. He held it in front of his mouth and paused. He scratched his bald head with his empty hand. "Wait, now I can't remember the dog's real name…such a strong little pooch. Protective, and fearless, too, like a little guard dog."

"Hmm, a guard dog?" Lola thought about it. "Was his name Rocky? Or Tiger? Or Champ?"

"Macho?" Lillian Jones guessed. "Or Wolf?"

"Ah, now I remember," said Grampa Ed. "His name was Cupcake."

Lola and her mom laughed. Grampa Ed laughed, too. He laughed so hard it turned into a cough. Lillian Jones patted her father on the back and handed him a glass of water.

When Grampa Ed stopped coughing, he took a deep breath. Then he popped another quesadilla wedge in his mouth.

Lillian Jones rose from the table. "Speaking of cupcakes…" She went to the counter and held up a box. "Who wants to bake some?"

Lola smiled a big smile with dimples at both ends. "*Glummy, wondercrump* cupcakes for dessert!" she squealed. "That means delicious, wonderful cupcake. Yes, please!"

Soon, Lillian Jones, Grampa Ed, and Lola cleared the table, washed their hands, and got ready to mix ingredients.

"Did you get a reward for finding Cupcake, Grampa?"

"Yes, we did!" he said. "Two dollars. That was pretty *wondercrump,* too."

4.
Doodle Dreams

Lola dreamed about a dog again that night. And the night after that.

In one dream, a goldendoodle baked Lola giant chocolate cupcakes. In the other dream, a schnoodle in a hat made of ten-dollar bills led Lola on an adventure over mountains and through caves filled with doggie dreams kept in little spice bottles.

The night before her class field trip to the animal shelter, Lola decided to read one more chapter of *The BFG* before turning out the lights. In *The BFG*, the Big Friendly Giant has a magic, trumpet-like instrument that he uses to blow lovely dreams into the bedrooms of sleeping children. Lola wished the BFG would blow her a dream about a friendly labradoodle...and a little while later she fell asleep with the book in her hands....

She dreamed about a labradoodle who blew a trumpet to play jazzy songs of heartache and love. But as she listened, the notes coming out of the trumpet turned into tiny helicopters (or *bellypoppers*, as the labradoodle called them). Lola

and the labradoodle flew to an animal shelter, where a little black-and-white dog greeted them, wagging its tail.

When she woke up the next morning, Lola was extra excited. She told Grampa Ed all about her latest dream as Grampa Ed slurped his coffee and worked on her pigtails.

"Grampa, do you think it's possible to choose your dreams?"

"I don't think so, kid. It's not TV."

"The BFG says dreams float around all the time like *wispy-misty* bubbles, searching for sleeping people. And last night I tried to dream about a labradoodle, and I did!"

"Probably a coincidence."

Grampa Ed slurped his coffee. "But you know what? When I was making all those crazy pigtails for you, I did dream about pigtails a couple of times. And when I first met your grandmother and then I had to leave home to join the Navy, I dreamed about her *all* the time. I looked forward to going to sleep every night because it was the only way I got to see her."

Lola turned and looked up. "Wow! So maybe if you're thinking a lot about something, you have a better chance of dreaming about it."

"That makes sense." Grampa Ed gently turned Lola's head and went back to work on the pigtails.

"That gives me an idea, Grampa," Lola said. "If I can get Mom to think happy thoughts about dogs right before she goes to sleep, maybe she'll have happy dog dreams, and then she'll want to get a dog!"

"I've heard worse plans than that one," Grampa Ed said.

"Really?"

"No. I was just being nice. That's the worst plan I've ever heard. Sorry, kid."

"What's wrong with it?"

"First of all, dreams are unpredictable. But even if you *can* change her dreams, that's not going to change her mind. And even if you change her mind, there's still a No Dogs Allowed rule in this building."

Lola rubbed her chin.

"You know what, Grampa. You're being too negative."

"Is that so?"

"Yes, it is. Have you read *The BFG?*"

"Oh sure, *The Baseball Field Guide?* I love that book."

"No, *The Big Friendly Giant!* In *The BFG,* this little girl named Sophie comes up with a practically impossible plan to stop the mean giants from eating children. But the Big Friendly Giant doesn't tell her it's a bad plan. You know what he does? He *helps* her!"

Grampa gently tapped Lola on the head to tell her the pigtails were done. "Fine, how can I help?"

Lola rubbed her chin.

"Can you draw me ten pictures of dogs? And can you have them finished when I get home from school?"

"Any kind of dog I want?"

"Any kind you want! No, wait! They have to be *friendly* dogs. No snarling ones. Oh, and no flames shooting out of their eyes, no missile launchers on their backs, and no brass knuckles on their paws!"

Grampa threw his hands toward the sky. "You're taking all the fun out of it, kid...but I'll do my best."

"Thanks, Grampa!" Lola kissed his cheek. "I love you!"

$\mathcal{elle}$

Before they boarded the bus to go to the animal shelter, Mrs. Gunderson asked her students to select books from the classroom's library. "You will each get to read a book to one of the animals. These animals don't get enough attention, and I think they would love to hear some good stories."

"I want to read *Harry Potter* to an otter!" said Sadie.

"I want to read *The Wizard of Oz* to an ostrich," said Celeste.

"I want to read *Le Petit Prince* to a French poodle," said Antoinette.

"I want to read *Peter Pan* to a crocodile," said Howie.

"I want to feed my math book to a lion," said Gabriel.

Laughter filled the room until Mrs. Gunderson interrupted.

29

"Children," she said. "I applaud your creativity! But this is an animal shelter, not a zoo. They have cats and dog, mostly, and perhaps a bunny rabbit or two. And you will not be permitted to choose your animal. The shelter will match you with an animal."

Lola closed her eyes and made a silent wish: "Please, please, *please*, let me get a dog! Any kind of dog! *Puh-leeeze!*"

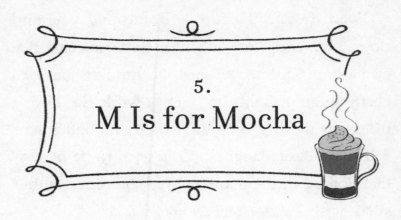

5.
M Is for Mocha

Lola and her classmates couldn't wait to see the animals and to read them stories. But first they met a volunteer from the shelter named Mr. Tibbs.

"Good morning, children," said Mr. Tibbs. "Before we go inside to see the animals, I'd like to tell you about the shelter. I'm a volunteer here. I help out because I love animals. I come in for a few hours every day to clean cages, mop floors, and spend time with my furry friends."

Mr. Tibbs was tall and thin and had neat silver hair. He wore splattered pants and a gray sweatshirt with holes in the elbows.

"Even though it's fun to be around cats and dogs," he said, "my job is messy. Animals pee and poop, and sometimes we humans have to clean up after them. It's a lot of work. So, I hope no one is wearing a fancy tuxedo or a ball gown."

The students laughed. Lola tried to be patient, like Sophie in the giant's cave. She repeated her silent wish: "*Puh-leeeze let me get a dog!*"

Mr. Tibbs told the class that when he first came to the shelter, he preferred dogs to cats. The dogs were always excited to see him. The dogs did tricks. "I was a little bit scared of cats, I must admit," he said. "But I learned how to socialize with them, and now I love cats." His voice lowered to a whisper. "Maybe even *more* than dogs."

Lola shook her head and thought: "*Puh-leeeze let me get a dog!*"

Mr. Tibbs continued: "Did you know there are more cats than dogs in American homes? Did you know cats usually live longer than dogs?"

"I don't want a cat! I want a *dog*! *A dog, dog, DOG!*"

Everyone turned and looked at Lola.

"Oopsies!" She felt her face flush with embarrassment. "I didn't mean to say that out loud! Sorry."

After Mr. Tibbs finished talking about being a good pet owner, he explained the rules for approaching and then petting animals.

Finally, he took the class into the part of the shelter where the animals waited in cages. Lola walked past the room with the cats and into the larger room where the dogs waited. She saw a cute pug that looked like a worried potato; a golden retriever with short fluffy ears that stuck out sideways; and a nervous chihuahua that strongly resembled Mr. Murch, her school's principal.

"Hello, cutie," Lola said, peering into the golden retriever's cage. "Would you like to hear a story?"

She felt a hand land gently on her shoulder and turned to see Mr. Tibbs smiling down at her.

"I have a very nice cat for you over here, young lady." He gestured to the row of cages in the former room.

Lola felt as if a big, gray cloud had covered the sun. Her shoulders drooped and her feet scraped the floor as she walked from the dog section to the cat section. Mr. Tibbs stopped in front of a cage. "This little guy came in yesterday," he said. "We haven't had a chance to name him yet."

Lola forced herself to look into the cage. When she did, she caught her breath. The little cat staring back at her was the most beautiful animal she had ever seen. It had light brown fur with dark brown stripes and pink ears and green eyes. The dark brown lines formed a little letter "M" on its forehead. The card on the cage read "Breed: TABBY." Lola let the cat sniff her fingers, as Mr.

Tibbs instructed the class on the field trip, and then she reached in to scratch the cat behind its ears. Its fur was so soft! The color reminded Lola of her mother's milky mocha coffee. At Lola's touch, the cat starting purring. It looked happy. It also looked like a cat that might enjoy a story. Lola took one last glance at the dog cages, sighed, and turned back to the cat.

"I hope you're not a scaredy-cat, because I'm going to read you a story about giants, O.K.? But don't worry. It's a happy story." She opened to page 89, where she had left off reading the night before. But then she worried that this cat might not want to start a story in the middle,

so she flipped back to the book's first page and began Chapter One. The cat leaned forward and straightened his ears. Lola felt certain the cat was listening.

"Since you don't have a

name, but you do have a letter 'M,' I'm going to call you Mocha. Do you like that?"

The cat stared calmly, as cats do. Lola read for a long time.

"Thanks for listening to the story, Mocha. You're pretty cool for a cat. I'm going to go look at dogs now, if you don't mind."

Mocha didn't really seem to mind, so off Lola went.

ell

Maya's mom walked the girls home from school that day. When Lola was dropped off at her building, she used the key that hung on a string around her neck to open the door to Grampa Ed's apartment on the first floor. Grampa Ed's apartment always smelled like paint and glue and coffee and Grampa, but today the smell of glue was extra strong.

"Knock-knock!" Lola shouted.

"Who's there?" Grampa shouted back.

"Felix!"

"Felix who?"

"Felix your face it means the dog likes you!"

"Hey, not bad, kid. I never heard that one before."

Grampa Ed was sitting at his desk working on a collage. He had drawn a picture of a dancing golden dog, and he had glued it to the center of the page, and then he had glued and drawn  more stuff around the dog: a matchbook from the Tic Toc Lounge, an ace of hearts from a deck of cards, a few lines of sheet music, a picture of a trumpet, and more. At the top of the page he wrote in big letters: *The Hound Dog Sang Lonely Dreams of Six-Fingered Blues.*

"Holy *snozzcumbers*, Grampa! This is beautiful! Is it for me? I wasn't expecting anything *this* beautiful! A plain old drawing of a dog would've been good enough."

"Oh, *now* you tell me!" Grampa rubbed his

bald head. "I've been working my fingers to the bone!"

"Hey, that's figurative language, Grampa!"

"If you say so."

"How many of these pictures did you make?"

"This one, plus four others. I know you said you wanted ten, but all this drawing and cutting and gluing takes time."

Grampa pulled out four more collages: Bird Dog, Taco Dog, Bathtub Dog, and Daisy Dog.

"I really wanted to give Daisy Dog a rocket launcher, but you asked me not to." Grampa shrugged. "Don't you think that would have been cool?"

"That *would* have been cool, Grampa. But these are perfect.

A rocket launcher might give Mom nightmares."

"Would you mind telling me why you wanted these pictures?"

"I'm going to use them to make Mom dream about dogs. I'm going to hang them all around the house. I might put one under her pillow, too."

"You never quit, do you, kid?"

"Of course not! Quitting is no fun!"

"Hey, how was the animal shelter? Did you find the dog of *your* dreams?"

"No." Lola frowned. "I had to read to a *cat*. He was a gorgeous cat, but still…"

"What did you read?"

"*The BFG.*"

"*The Big Farty Grampa*?"

"Grampa! Quit being *disgusting*!"

Grampa laughed. "But I can't quit. Quitting is no fun!"

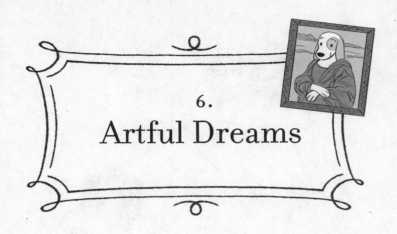

6.
Artful Dreams

After dinner that night, Lola and her mother had a pajama-and-popcorn-karaoke-dance party. They took turns picking songs. They sang and danced until they were sweaty and exhausted. They laughed so hard their stomachs hurt.

"I love to dance with you, Lola!" her mother said.

"Me, too. But can I tell you a secret, Mom?" Lola's brow sparkled with sweat.

"Of course!"

"I love dancing, but I don't like dancing in front of other people...except you."

41

"Me, too!" Lola's mother took a sip of water.

"Oh, good. I thought I was weird. I mean, if you love to do something, why should you be embarrassed?"

"Maybe even though we love to do something, we're worried about not being good at it," Lillian Jones said. "Maybe we should be more confident."

"I'm confident in my dreams!" Lola said.

"Me, too!" Lillian said, laughing. "And, right now, I'm confident you should brush your teeth. It's getting late!"

Lola ran to the bathroom first. She brushed her teeth quickly, tiptoed to her room to get the dog collages, and then tiptoed into her mother's room. She put the Daisy Dog picture under her mother's pillow. She hung the Dancing Dog on the door of her mother's closet, and the Bathtub Dog on the mirror in the bathroom. She put the Bird Dog in her mother's pajama drawer and the Taco Dog inside a box of chocolate-chip cookies in case her mother had a snack before bedtime.

~~~~

The next morning was a Saturday. Lola slept late. When she went into the kitchen, her mother was drinking her mocha coffee, eating yogurt, and reading the newspaper. Lola gave her mother a hug, and her mother kissed the top of Lola's head.

"Oh, Lola," Lillian Jones said. "I had the strangest dream last night!"

Lola's eyes opened wide. "Really?"

"You and I were in an art museum, and someone had replaced all the famous paintings with pictures of dogs. There was a picture of dogs in white wigs signing the Declaration of Independence. There was a picture of two dogs in front of a farm house, with one of them wearing overalls and holding a pitchfork. There was another picture

of lonely dogs sitting at a restaurant counter in a late-night diner, eating with forks and knives. In the dream, we were confused, so we went to the museum's information desk, where we were met by a big dog in a handsome blue uniform. When I asked him why all the paintings had dogs in them, he said it wasn't his job to comment on the meaning of the art."

Lola's mother sipped her coffee and shook her head.

"Such a strange dream!"

"Wow, that *is* a strange dream, Mom." Lola took out a box of cereal and a bowl. "Does it make you want to get a dog?"

"No, but it makes me want to go to the museum. Care to join me today? We could ride our bikes there."

"O.K.," Lola said. "I bet we'll see cute dogs on the bike path."

A few minutes later, Grampa Ed came upstairs to join Lola and her mother for breakfast. Lola made him a cup of coffee just the way he liked it.

"How did your plan work out last night?" he asked Lola.

Lola's mother looked up from her newspaper. "Plan?"

Lola pulled her grampa's arm and led him out of the kitchen. She whispered: "It worked! She had dog dreams! But they were strange dog dreams, not sweet ones."

"I *knew* I should've put a rocket launcher on Daisy Dog's back!"

"No, Grampa! It wasn't your fault."

"Oh, that's a relief." He smiled and slurped his coffee.

"But we have to keep trying. Can you make me more dog pictures?"

"How many?"

"Five more!"

"When do you need them?"

"Tonight, of course! There's no time to waste!"

"I'm going to need more coffee."

"You got it, Grampa!" She hugged him. "Coming right up!"

After breakfast, Lola and her mother got dressed and went to the basement to make sure their bicycles had enough air in the tires. Lola's tires were a little soft, so she pumped them up. Her mother's tires were fine.

Lola loved pumping bike tires even more than

she loved making coffee. The pump made a fun hissing noise, and she had to push with all of her weight to make the handle go down as the tires inflated.

A few minutes later, Lola and her mother, in matching helmets, were on the lakefront bicycle path, pedaling south toward the museum, with a soft wind at their backs. The sun rose high over the city's jagged skyline and the lake was shining like a sapphire.

Lola was proud of her bike-riding skills, and she carefully steered with one hand and pointed out dogs walking with their owners with her other hand.

"Do you like that dalmatian with the spots, Mom? What about the boxer?"

She couldn't hear her mother's response.

"Oooh, Mom, what about that big sheepdog?! Wouldn't it be fun to have a dog and take it to the park? Oh, look at that cute little dachshund!"

7.
Hatching a Plan

Each day for the next three days Lola hung Grampa's dog pictures around the house, and each day Lola's mother dreamed about dogs. On Sunday night Lillian Jones dreamed that she and a French poodle were eating toast. On Monday night she dreamed that she and four bulldogs were playing basketball against a team of bobcats.

"Don't these dreams make you wish you had a dog?" Lola asked her mother one night at dinner.

"No." Her mother took a bite of salad. "The dreams are nice. But when I wake up, I remember that dogs are expensive, they're a lot of work, and they make smelly poop that someone has to pick up... and that *someone* is going to be me most of the time."

Lola put down her fork. "But, Mom," she said, "the shelter will spay or neuter a dog for free! And the first check-up is free, too! That will save a lot of money! And then we could give a dog a 'forever home.' That's what Mr. Tibbs called it. You wouldn't have to do any work. I'd do everything! Even cleaning up the poop!"

"It's more work than you think, honey."

"I know it's a lot of work, Mom. They told us at the shelter. You have to feed the dog and brush its fur and give it a bath and take it for walks. You have to vacuum the fur when it gets on the couch or on the floor. You have to take the dog to the vet when it's sick. I can do *all* that!"

"I'm not so sure."

Lola looked at Grampa Ed, hoping he would offer support.

"Grampa, don't you think I can take care of a dog?"

"What?" Grampa looked up.

"Didn't you hear what we were saying?" Lola asked.

"Not really." He returned his gaze to his salad bowl. "Sorry. I was concentrating on my salad. It tastes pretty good, especially those round yellow things. I forget what they're called. But there are too many little parts in salad. Maybe I should put the whole thing in a blender and chug...."

"Grampa...." Lola gently interrupted. "We were talking about dogs. Don't you think I'm old enough to take care of a dog?"

"Sure. Whatever you say." He stabbed his fork into the salad bowl.

Lola turned back to Lillian. "Mom, is there *anything* I can do to change your mind?"

"I don't think so," her mother said.

Lola rubbed her chin.

"Uh-oh." Grampa Ed looked up from his bowl.

"What's the matter, Grampa? Did another

garbanzo bean escape from your fork?"

"Garbanzo bean! That's it! But no." Grampa took a bite. "I said 'uh-oh' because when Lola rubs her chin, it usually means she's hatching a new plan."

Lola *was* hatching a new plan. She hurried home from school the next day.

"Grampa!" She stepped up to Grampa Ed's drawing table. "Do you remember I told you that I went to the animal shelter and read a story to a cat?"

"Of course. You read that book called *The BFG...Bananas For Grampa....*"

"*The Big Friendly Giant*...oh, never mind. Anyway, I just realized something awful. I never finished reading the book to Mocha. And now that poor little kitty is probably having nightmares about giants sneaking around at night and stealing animals from their cages. Oh, Grampa, I just *have* to go back!"

Grampa gave a shrug.

Lola tapped her foot.

"Oh." Grampa made a scraping noise with his throat that wasn't pleasant. "You mean *now*?"

Lola smiled a tiny bit.

"You mean you want *me* to take you? *Now*?"

Lola smiled bigger.

As he rose from his chair, Grampa sang the first few words of the song that inspired the tattoo on his left arm: "*Whatever Lola wants, Lola gets....*"

Lola wrapped her arms around him and kissed his fuzzy cheek.

"Thank you, Grampa! You're the best! *The Best, Funnest Grampa* of them all!"

"The BFG?"

"The BFG!"

8.
A Black-and-White Dog Appears...Again!

The big city glittered in bright sunlight as Lola and Grampa Ed rode the bus downtown, passing soccer fields and schools and stores and restaurants and busy people coming and going.

Lola, still dressed in her blue school uniform, liked the feeling of riding the bus with Grampa. She wished she could open the window and hear the city's noises and smell its smells, but the window didn't open. She thought of all the animals in the shelter and wondered if they ever got to go outside. Maybe the dogs, probably not the cats.

"Hello, Mr. Tibbs," said Lola when they reached the shelter. "Do you remember me? My name is Lola, and I was here with my class the other day. This my grandfather."

Mr. Tibbs stood up from the reception desk and shook Grampa Ed's hand first and Lola's hand second.

"I do remember you, Lola," he said. "You read a story to the new tabby."

"That's right! Is that cat still here?"

"Yes, he is. Have you come in to adopt him?"

"No, I came to read to him again. I felt bad that I didn't finish the book last time."

"Yes, of course." Mr. Tibbs picked up the keys from his desk and led the way. "I'm sure he'd like that."

Lola held Grampa Ed's hand as they walked. When they got inside, Lola knelt on the floor, said hello to Mocha, and opened her book. While Lola read to the cat, Mr. Tibbs showed Grampa around the shelter.

Mocha loved *The BFG*. He paid attention to every word. When Lola got to the end of a chapter and closed the book, Mocha meowed and reached a paw through the bars of his cage to get Lola's attention, so Lola read another chapter. As long as Lola read, Mocha sat perfectly still. But when Lola once again reached the end of a chapter and closed the book, the same thing happened. Mocha meowed and reached a paw through the bars of the cage.

"I know! The story's getting exciting, isn't it, Mocha? But I have to go now!"

Meow! Meow!

"O.K., O.K.! One more chapter."

Lola and Mocha couldn't stop. The book got so exciting they *had* to finish it. When she got to the end, Lola stood up, reached a finger into Mocha's cage, and scratched him behind his ears.

"You really liked that, didn't you, Mocha? I was worried you might be scared. Or you might be confused because the BFG uses a lot of funny words." Lola paused. "But maybe they sound perfectly normal to you. Maybe they're not all *jumbly* and *hopscotchy* to a cat!"

Just then, Mocha turned his head slightly, and so did Lola, as a little black-and-white dog scampered across the floor, with Mr. Tibbs rushing to catch him. Every time the dog stopped running and Mr. Tibbs bent to pick it up, the little dog took off again. That made Grampa Ed laugh. Lola's mouth and eyes opened wide. It was the little black-and-white dog from her dream!

The one she saw from her window!

"Here, doggie!" Lola called. She put out her hand for the dog to sniff just as Mr. Tibbs had instructed the class on the field trip. The little dog stopped and sniffed Lola's hand. Lola bent over and stroked the fur on the dog's back. "Well, hello, cutie!" The little black-and-white dog jumped to lick her face.

"He's adorable!" Lola said, laughing.

"It's a *she*," Mr. Tibbs said.

Mr. Tibbs scooped up the dog in his arms and thanked Lola for helping to catch her. As Mr. Tibbs carried the dog back to her cage, the dog twisted around to get a last look at Lola and Grampa Ed. One of her ears flopped one way, and one flopped the other way.

"That's the dog from my dream, Grampa!" Lola squealed. "Isn't she cute?"

Grampa Ed had a big smile on his face as he watched the antics of the little dog. "Very cute!"

When Lola looked up at Mocha again, the cat was out of sight, curled up in the back of his cage.

Before they left, Mr. Tibbs gave Lola and Grampa Ed a pamphlet that explained the rules for animal adoption.

"We have a rule in our building," Grampa Ed said. "No dogs allowed."

"Sometimes those rules can be changed," Mr. Tibbs said with a smile.

Lola was quiet as she and Grampa Ed boarded the bus and rode him.

"Are you O.K., kid?" Grampa asked.

"Yes," Lola said. "Just thinking."

"About dogs?"

"Actually, cats. Or *one* cat. I think I hurt Mocha's feelings."

"You're not falling in love with that kitty, are you, kid? I thought you were a dog person!"

"No, Grampa. But cats have feelings, too, you know."

Grampa put a big arm around Lola's shoulders as the big city bus carried them home.

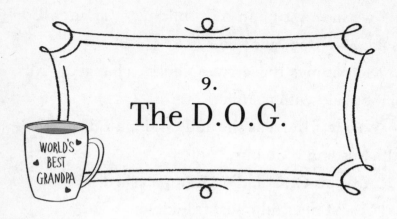

9.
The D.O.G.

The next morning was Saturday. On Saturdays Grampa Ed made chocolate-chip pancakes, Lola made coffee, and Lola's mother slept late.

"I had the strangest dream last night," Grampa Ed said as he stirred the batter.

"Uh-oh." Lola spilled a little coffee as she carried Grampa's mug.

"I dreamed about that little black-and-white dog that escaped from her cage yesterday. I dreamed she followed us home on the bus and hid in my closet. When I opened the closet door to put away my shoes, the dog was in there with a rocket-launcher on her back. When I asked her if she was planning to fire rockets, she winked and said, 'Don't worry, Ed, I would never fire a rocket launcher at anyone. I only carry it to scare away giant garbanzo beans.'"

Lola laughed.

Grampa laughed, too. "I probably should have mentioned that it was a talking dog."

"A talking dog with a rocket launcher!" Lola laughed. "And giant garbanzo beans! Did the dream make you want to get a dog?"

"It made me want to get a rocket launcher!" Grampa Ed made a big slurping sound with his coffee. "I have to admit, though, I liked that silly little pooch from the shelter. All this talk about dogs got me thinking. I'm home all day. I wouldn't mind having a little pooch to keep me company while I'm drawing and painting."

"Are you serious, Grampa?"

"Sure, I'm serious. But the building has a rule, so it doesn't matter."

"Grampa, I've been wondering. There are only three apartments in our building—yours, mine and Mom's, and Ms. Miller's upstairs. Maybe we could vote to change the rule!"

"Maybe. But I think we'd have to get everyone to agree. It would have to be a unanimous vote."

Lola couldn't believe what she was hearing! If Grampa got a dog, she could play with it and help take care of it and then she could prove to her mother that she was responsible enough to get her *own* dog. Even if she had to wait until she was a little older, it wouldn't be too bad. Grampa's dog would be part of her family.

"Oh my gosh! Grampa! You know what I just realized? If you got a dog, it would The Dog of Grampa. *The D.O.G.!* Oh, Grampa, I hope Ms. Miller says yes!"

10.
True Friends
Are Like Fingers

As they walked to school on Monday, Lola told Maya and Fayth about her visit to the dog shelter.

"My grampa might get a dog! A cute little black-and-white one. She escaped from her cage at the shelter and she wouldn't stop running. I think she was scared. But when I put out my hand, she stopped and sniffed and jumped up to lick my face! And Grampa was smiling and laughing the whole time that dog was with us. I really hope Grampa gets that dog!"

"But I thought you wanted a labradoodle," Fayth said.

"I do, but this dog is *really, really* cute. And friendly and funny. And she needs a home."

"But what about No Dogs Allowed in your building?" Maya asked. "Are you going to say phooey to rules?"

The girls laughed.

"Mr. Tibbs at the animal shelter said those rules can change sometimes," Lola said. "I'm going to ask my mom and Ms. Miller, our upstairs neighbor, if they'll vote to change the rule."

"Oh, can we make a petition like we did when we wanted to change the school dress code?" Fayth asked.

"I don't think a petition will help because we don't have enough people in our building." Lola rubbed her chin. "But...I have an idea for how you can help me!"

Maya and Fayth always helped Lola. And Lola always helped Maya and Fayth. As Mrs. Gunderson said: True friends are like fingers; they can always be counted on.

"You guys both have dogs. What if we got letters from the people in your building who *don't* have dogs, letters that said they didn't mind having dogs in the building. And then we could show those letters to my mom and Ms. Miller to make sure they'll vote for allowing dogs."

"That's a terrific idea!" Maya said.

Fayth nodded. "And I can bring my dog with us when we give the letters to your mom and Ms. Miller. When they meet Queenie, they'll love dogs even more!"

"And I can bring my dog, Wrigley!" Maya said.

"Great plan!" Lola said.

In school that day, Mrs. Gunderson continued teaching the class about poetry.

"Today we're going to talk about narrative poetry," Ms. Gunderson said. "That means poetry that tells a story. A narrative poem has characters and conflict and action, just like other stories. It can also have figurative language. And it should be fun."

Ms. Gunderson handed out a few examples of narrative poems and asked the students to write their own. Lola started right away.

RIDING THE BUS TO GET A DOG
By Lola Jones

It's Saturday and I'm wearing gray leggings

and a gray T-shirt, and my mother calls it a groutfit

because it's all gray.

The sky is gray too.

But I don't care because we're riding the bus

to the animal shelter to get a dog.

We walk into the shelter,

an ocean of gray cement and gray cages,

And we see a black-and-white dog

as sad as a gift-wrapped box

torn open and it turns out to be empty.

We sign the papers and take the dog home

and open a can of dog food

and we all live happy as sunshine.

Arf! Arf! Thanks for reading Lola's poem!

At the bottom of her poem, Lola drew a picture of a little black-and-white dog. She drew a word balloon coming from the dog's mouth and inside the balloon, she wrote: *"Arf! Arf! Thanks for reading Lola's poem!"*

ℓℓℓ

After school, Lola, Maya, and Fayth knocked on doors, first in Maya's building, and then in Fayth's. They got six letters from neighbors who said dogs were loyal and protective and nice to have in the building. Maya's father called the letters *testimonials*, which is a fancy word for a written declaration for something you like. Lola loved fancy words.

When they got back to Lola's house, it was almost dinnertime. Maya and Wrigley and Fayth and Queenie went to Grampa Ed's apartment first to tell him their plan.

"Tell your dogs not to bark!" Lola turned to her friends as they reached the door.

Both dogs barked.

"Do they bark whenever they hear the word *bark*?" Lola frowned.

Both dogs barked again.

"I said don't bark!"

Bark!

The girls cracked up.

"Tell your dogs to be quiet," Lola whispered.

The dogs didn't bark.

First, they talked to Grampa Ed. From Grampa's apartment they walked upstairs to Ms. Celia Miller's apartment on the third floor. Lola was so nervous her legs wobbled on the stairs. What if Ms. Miller hated dogs? What if Ms. Miller's cat hated dogs? What if they fought like cats and dogs? Would that still count as figurative language if the cat and dogs *actually* fought?

Lola took a deep breath and knocked.

"Who is it?"

"Hi, Ms. Miller, it's me, Lola. Before you open the door, I need to know if you and your cat are afraid of dogs!"

"Hi, Lola. No, I'm not afraid of dogs. Ginger is, but she hides under the bed when she's scared. Why?"

"Oh, great! I'm here with my friends and they brought their dogs. You can open the door now."

Ms. Miller opened her door. Ginger was nowhere to be seen. Lola introduced Maya and Fayth and their dogs. Lola told Ms. Miller that Grampa Ed wanted to get a dog, but he could only get one if everyone in the building agreed to change the no-dogs-allowed rule. Lola showed Ms. Miller the testimonials from the neighbors of Maya and Fayth who liked having dogs around.

"These are excellent testimonials, Lola," Ms. Miller said. "You and Maya and Fayth did good work. So did Wrigley and Queenie."

"So, will you vote to change the rule?"

"Yes, I will," Ms. Miller said.

Lola and her friends cheered.

"But..." Ms. Miller continued. "I think we ought to make a new rule: no more than one dog per apartment. We don't want too many animals, do we?"

"That sounds fair, Ms. Miller! Thanks!"

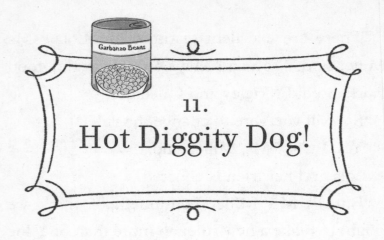

11.
Hot Diggity Dog!

Lola and Grampa Ed cooked chili for dinner.

"Do you want to add garbanzo beans?" Lola held up a can.

"Sure." A tear ran down Grampa Ed's cheek as he chopped onions. "And we'll make the chili nice and thick so they can't run away."

"Let's make it spicy, too!" Lola said.

"That reminds of a joke," Grampa Ed said. "A guy walks into the doctor's office. He's got jalapeno pepper stuck in one nostril, a clove of garlic in the other nostril, and a banana stuck in one ear. He says, 'Doc, this is terrible! What's wrong with me?' The doctor says, 'First of all, you're not eating right…'"

Lola paused. "I don't get it."

"Never mind." Grampa laughed. "What do you get when you cross a chili pepper, a shovel, and a German shepherd?

"I don't know," Lola said.

"A hot diggity dog!"

"That one's a lot better," Lola said. "And speaking of dogs, guess what? Ms. Miller said she would vote to change the No Dogs Allowed rule! So, if Mom says she'll vote to change it too, you can get that cute little black-and-white dog. And maybe I can get one, too!"

The lock on the front door clicked, and Lola sprinted down the hall to greet her mother with a big hug.

"Ms. Celia Miller said she'll vote *yes* to dogs! And Grampa said yes. Will you say yes, too, Mom? *Will* you?"

"Whoa! Let me take off my jacket, sweetie." Lillian Jones laughed. "Let's talk about it over dinner, O.K.? How was your day?"

"My day was great!" Lola said, and she told her mother all about her narrative poem and her visit to Ms. Miller's.

Everyone worked together getting dinner ready. When they were done, Lola carried the steaming hot bowls of chili to the table while her mother filled the water glasses, and Grampa Ed put out napkins and silverware.

Lola waited patiently until everyone had taken a bite before asking her mother again: "Mom, will you *please* vote yes to dogs in our building?"

"Oh, wow, this chili is spicy!" Lola's mother took another bite. "And delicious."

"Well?"

Lola's mother sipped from her water glass. "If your Grampa wants a dog and if Ms. Miller says it's O.K., then it's O.K. with me.

I still don't think a dog is right for us. But Grampa can do whatever he wants."

Lola smiled and looked at Grampa Ed. Grampa Ed smiled back.

"You know, kid, I'm going to need help with that pooch. And I think she really likes you."

"Oh, Grampa, are you sure that little black-and-white dog is still available? What if she's already been adopted?"

Grampa loaded his spoon with a mountain of chili and tilted it back and forth and side to side to see if the garbanzo beans stayed in place. They did. He chewed and gulped and made a big *aaaah*.

"I already called the shelter and told them I'd take that dog." Grampa took another huge bite. "I had a feeling this story would have a happy ending." He hummed the song "Whatever Lola Wants."

"Oh, I'm so happy! We're going to have The D.O.G.! *The Dog of Grampa!* Thank you, Mom! Thank you, Grampa! Oh, Grampa! I have a long

list of dog names. Mom, may I go to my room and get it?"

"Sorry, kid," Grampa said. "I already picked a name."

"You did? What is it?"

"You'll see."

"Yulesee? You're going to name your dog Yulesee? What kind of a name is *that*? That's even worse than Ten Dollars!"

Grampa Ed laughed

"You'll see," he said. "You…will…see."

12.
Going Home

"What's that new book you're reading?" Lola's mother asked.

Lola and her mother and Grampa Ed were riding the bus downtown to the animal shelter to pick up Grampa's new dog.

"It's called *No Flying in the House*." Lola thumbed the pages of the book. "It's about a girl named Annabel Tippens who has a tiny dog instead of parents. I think it's going to be my new favorite book, and it has a cat in it, so I thought I'd read to Mocha."

"Who's Mocha?" Lillian asked.

"A beautiful cat at the shelter," Lola said. "He was new and didn't have a name, so I named after your mocha coffee. He's the same color."

"That's nice that you want to read to him," Lillian Jones said.

"He's a great listener." Lola smiled.

Lola's mother looked at Grampa Ed and smiled. Grampa Ed smiled back. Then they looked out the window at the green expanse of a crowded park.

At the shelter, Grampa had to fill out dog adoption paperwork, which gave Lola time to read her book to Mocha. After the first chapter, Lola's mother read Chapter Two.

"I can't believe how well this cat pays attention!" Lola's mother said. "You were right!"

"I know! He loved *The BFG!* The scary parts didn't scare him at all."

Mocha meowed and stretched a paw through the bars of his cage.

"O.K., sorry, Mocha." Lola's mother stroked Mocha's outstretched paw and turned to the beginning of Chapter Two. "Back to the story...."

Mocha listened and purred.

Finally, Grampa returned with his little black-and-white dog on a new red leash and the biggest smile Lola had ever seen on his face.

"Ladies," he said, "meet the D.O.G.! Her name is Garbo! That's short for Garbanzo."

"Oh, my gosh!" Lola kneeled to stroke the fur on the dog's back. "I love that name, Grampa! It's perfect!"

Lillian put out her hand and let the dog sniff her. "So cute!"

"Is everybody ready to go?" Grampa asked.

"Oh, Grampa, may I please hold the leash?" Lola paused. "Wait! I forgot about Mocha! We can't leave until we finish reading Chapter Two! *Please, Mom?*"

Mocha's gaze was on Garbo. "Don't worry," Lola said to the cat. "Garbo's on a leash this time." Then she reached a finger into Mocha's cage and scratched behind his ear reassuringly.

"O.K., you read it to him." Lola's mother smiled and walked away with Grampa Ed and Garbo. "We'll leave you and Mocha alone."

Lola finished reading the chapter just as her mother returned.

"I think Mocha likes *No Flying in the House* even more than *The BFG*," Lola said. "Probably because it has a cat. I have to come back soon so I can read him the rest of the story."

"No, you don't," Lillian's mother said.

"Yes, I *do*, Mom!" Lola looked up at her mother. "It would be impolite not to. And Mocha needs attention and…" Lola stopped. "Mom…why are you smiling?"

"Because you don't have to come back. Mocha's coming with *you*! We're taking Mocha home!"

Lola gasped. Tears filled her eyes and poured down her cheeks. She had never cried happy tears before and she wanted to stop but she couldn't. She could hardly speak.

"Oh, Mom!" She hugged her mother with all her might.

Mocha meowed and reached both paws through the bars of his cage, snagging Lola's sleeve in one, and Lillian's sleeve in the other.

Soon they were back on the bus headed north, Grampa Ed with Garbo curled quietly at his feet, and Lola with Mocha in a carton on her lap. The sun was setting behind the glass and brick buildings that raced by.

Lola didn't say a word all the way home. Finally, as the view outside the window grew more familiar and the passing city streets felt more like her own, she realized she wasn't dreaming. She was going home with two people who loved her and two new pets to love.

She leaned on her mother's shoulder and spoke softly in her ear: "*Whoopsey-splunkers….*"

"What, sweetie?"

"It means *Wow!*"